LIBRARY
ANDERSON ELEMENTARY

CAN YOU HEAR ME, GRANDAD?

by
Pat Thomson
Illustrated by
Jez Alborough

Delacorte Press/New York

Hello, Grandad.
We are going to have a treat.
We're going to the zoo.

What's that? Glue?
You've fallen in the glue?
Never mind. Just don't sit down
and you'll be all right.

Not glue, Grandad, zoo.
We're going to the zoo.
We'll probably go on the train.

Go on a crane?
That's unusual.
It will be handy for elephant rides.
Elephants are very high up.

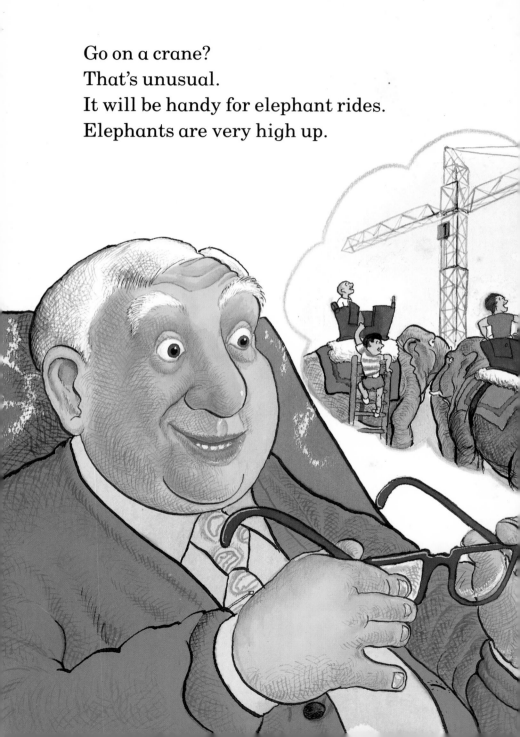

Not crane, Grandad, train.
Are you a bit deaf today,
or are you teasing?
Mom says I must sit beside her.

Sit on a tiger? Your Mom?
Isn't she amazing!
What a brave woman.

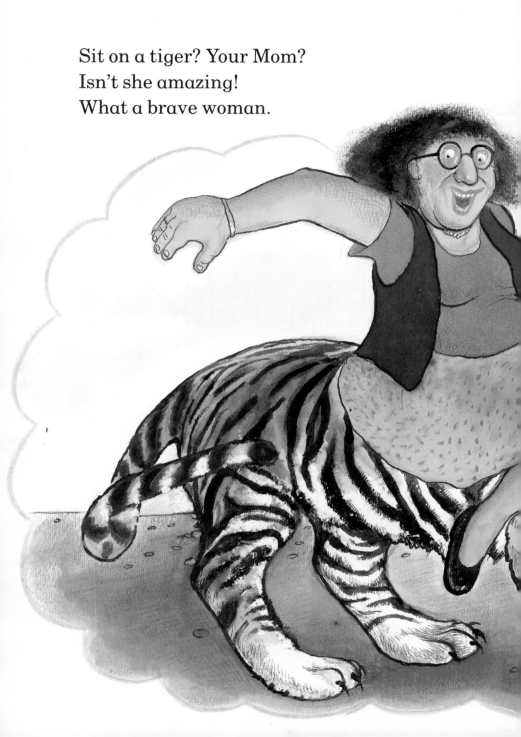

Not a tiger, Grandad, beside her.
I must sit beside her on the train.
We're going to have some tea.

Going to see the flea?
Do they have fleas in zoos these days?
You can borrow my glasses, if you like.

Not flea, Grandad, tea.
Mom wants to see the leopards.
She told me there's a saying,
"A leopard cannot change its spots."

Cannot change its socks?
Phew! That's terrible.
It must be dreadful in hot weather.

Not socks, Grandad, spots.
You are trying to make me laugh.
Did you know that lions and leopards
are called the big cats?

Wear big hats, do they?
It's to keep the sun off, no doubt.
They come from very hot countries.

Not big hats, Grandad, big cats.
They belong to the cat family.
I learned that at school.

Leaned over the pool?
The sea lion pool?
If you fall in,
I'll come and feed you with fish.

Not pool, Grandad, school.
I won't fall in.
I don't want a fish moustache
like the sea lions.
I shall go for a ride.
You can even ride on the llamas.

Go in your pajamas?
What next!
I hope there are no
holes in them.

Not pajamas, Grandad, llamas.
I'm not going to show
everyone my pajamas.
I'll go and see the parrots,
I'd like to see them flying around.

Carrots flying around?
You must keep your head down.
You don't want to be knocked out
by a carrot.

Not carrots, Grandad, parrots.
Do you think we'll see
the giant anteater?

Giant aunt-eater?
Must be big.
I doubt if it could swallow
your Auntie Mabel.

Not aunt-eater, Grandad, anteater.
I'll go and see the bears, too.
They live in a cave.

Give them a shave?
Why do you want to do that?
Bears don't know where their
coats end and their beards begin.

Cave, Grandad, not shave.
You are a terrible tease today.
Well, I like all the animals
but I think I like the monkeys best.

You'd like to be the monkeys' guest?
Yes, you would like that.
Up there in the trees,
monkeying around.
I expect you will enjoy your visit.

Mom asked if you would like
to come too.
Would you like to come
to the zoo with us?

105
ANDERSON ELEMENTARY SCHOOL
LIBRARY

My goodness, how clearly you speak
for someone so young.
Yes, I'd love to come.
I want to see the reindeer,
so I'd better fetch my umbrella.